Margaret Mayo   illustrated by Alex Ayliffe

STOMP, DINOSAUR, STOMP!

Walker & Company New York

Mighty Tyrannosaurus

loved stomp, stomp, stomping,
gigantic legs striding, enormous jaws opening,

jagged teeth waiting for guzzle, guzzling!

So stomp, Tyrannosaurus, stomp!

Immense Diplodocus

loved swish, swish, swishing,

long tail **flicking** and fast whip, **whipping**,

enemy **surprising** and—*smack!*—**scaring.**

So **swish,** Diplodocus, **swish!**

Crested Pteranodon

loved glide, glide, gliding, spreading wide wings, circling, rising,

higher and higher, swooping and soaring.

So glide, Pteranodon, glide!

Fierce Velociraptor

loved hunt, **hunt, hunting,**

in fearsome packs **running, racing,**

hooked claws ready for quick **pouncing.**

So **hunt**, Velociraptor, **hunt!**

Sleek Plesiosaurus

loved zoom, zoom, zooming,
sturdy paddles swooshing, flapping,

neck lunging, teeth showing—**snatch!**—fish **trapping.**

So **zoom**, Plesiosaurus, **zoom!**

Tough Ankylosaurus

loved whack, **whack**, **whacking,**

tail-club **swinging,** battles **winning,**

while hiding safely under spikes and armor plating.

So whack, Ankylosaurus, whack!

Massive Brachiosaurus

loved gulp, gulp, gulping,

leaves **picking,** mouth **stuffing** . . . no **chewing!**

Fast **eating,** hungry, hungry giant . . . more food needing.

So **gulp,** Brachiosaurus, **gulp!**

Wrinkly Triceratops

loved charge, **charge, charging,**
thumpety-thump! Huge feet **pounding,**

horns jutting, and—wham!—head-butting.

So charge, Triceratops, charge!

Stiff-tailed Iguanodon

loved chomp, **chomp, chomping,**

tough plants **grabbing, cutting,** and **biting,**

chewing, mashing, and noisy **grinding.**

So **chomp,** Iguanodon, **chomp!**

Feathered Oviraptor

loved guard, **guard**, **guarding**,

soft sand **shaping**, snug nest **making**,

eggs protecting, until—cric-crac!—babies hatching.

So guard, Oviraptor, guard!

Fantastic Stegosaurus

loved stroll, **stroll, strolling,**

tiny eyes glaring, spiky tail **waving,**

showing off big curvy plates . . . and looking quite amazing!

So stroll, Stegosaurus, stroll!

Imagine the creatures in a grand parade—

with no fighting allowed and no one afraid!

Some **plodding,** some **swooping,** while others just **romp,**

and Tyrannosaurus leading . . .

STOMP! STOMP! STOMP!

Ankylosaurus
an-ki-loh-sore-us

Iguanodon
ig-wah-noh-don

Triceratops
try-seh-ra-tops

Brachiosaurus
brak-ee-oh-sore-us

Velociraptor
vel-oss-uh-rap-tor

Plesiosaurus
plee-see-oh-sore-us